Mark Twain

The Jumping Frog

卡城名蛙

U0106941

商務印書館

出版説明

　　本館一向倡導優質閱讀，近年來連續推出了以 "Q" 為標識的 "Quality English Learning 優質英語學習" 系列，其中《讀名著學英語》叢書，更是香港書展入選好書，讀者反響令人鼓舞。推動社會閱讀風氣，推動英語經典閱讀，藉閱讀拓廣世界視野，提高英語水平，已經成為一種潮流。

　　然良好閱讀習慣的養成非一日之功，大多數初、中級程度的讀者，常視直接閱讀厚重的原著為畏途。如何給年輕的讀者提供切實的指引和幫助，如何既提供優質的學習素材，又提供名師的教學方法，是當下社會關注的重要問題。 針對這種情況，本館特別延請香港名校名師，根據多年豐富的教學經驗，精選海外適合初、中級英語程度讀者的優質經典讀物，有系統地出版了這套叢書，名為《Black Cat 優質英語階梯閱讀》。

　　《Black Cat 優質英語階梯閱讀》體現了香港名校名師堅持經典學習的教學理念，以及多年行之有效的學習方法。既有經過改寫和縮寫的經典名著，又有富創意的現代作品；既有精心設計的聽、説、讀、寫綜合練習，又有豐富的歷史文化知識；既有彩色插圖、繪圖和照片，又有英美專業演員朗讀作品的 CD。適合口味不同的讀者享受閱讀之樂，欣賞經典之美。

　　《Black Cat 優質英語階梯閱讀》由淺入深，逐階提升，好像參與一個尋寶遊戲，入門並不難，但要真正尋得寶藏，需要投入，更需要堅持。只有置身其中的人，才能體味純正英語的魅力，領略得到真寶的快樂。當英語閱讀成為自己生活的一部分，英語水平的提高自然水到渠成。

商務印書館 (香港) 有限公司
編輯部

使用説明

1 應該怎樣選書？

按閱讀興趣選書

《Black Cat 優質英語階梯閱讀》精選世界經典作品，也包括富於創意的現代作品；既有膾炙人口的小説、戲劇，又有非小説類的文化知識讀物，品種豐富，內容多樣，適合口味不同的讀者挑選自己感興趣的書，享受閱讀的樂趣。

按英語程度選書

《Black Cat 優質英語階梯閱讀》現設 Level 1 至 Level 6，由淺入深，涵蓋初、中級英語程度。讀物分級採用了國際上通用的劃分標準，主要以詞彙（vocabulary）和結構（structures）劃分。

Level 1 至 Level 3 出現的詞彙較淺顯，相對深的核心詞彙均配上中文解釋，節省讀者查找詞典的時間，以專心理解正文內容。在註釋的幫助下，讀者若能流暢地閱讀正文內容，就不用擔心這一本書程度過深。

Level 1 至 Level 3 出現的動詞時態形式和句子結構比較簡單。動詞時態形式以現在時（present simple）、現在時進行式（present continuous）、過去時（past simple）為主，句子結構大部分是簡單句（simple sentences）。此外，還包括比較級和最高級（comparative and superlative forms）、可數和不可數名詞（countable and uncountable nouns）以及冠詞（articles）等語法知識點。

Level 4 至 Level 6 出現的動詞時態形式，以現在完成時（present perfect）、現在完成時進行式（present perfect continuous）、過去完成時（past perfect continuous）為主，句子結構大部分是複合句（compound sentences）、條件從句（1st and 2nd conditional sentences）等。此外，還包括情態動詞（modal verbs）、被動形式（passive forms）、動名詞

(gerunds)、短語動詞（phrasal verbs）等語法知識點。

根據上述的語法範圍，讀者可按自己實際的英語水平，如詞彙量、語法知識、理解能力、閱讀能力等自主選擇，不再受制於學校年級劃分或學歷高低的約束，完全根據個人需要選擇合適的讀物。

② 怎樣提高閱讀效果？

閱讀的方法主要有兩種：一是泛讀，二是精讀。兩者各有功能，適當地結合使用，相輔相成，有事半功倍之效。

泛讀，指閱讀大量適合自己程度（可稍淺，但不能過深）、不同內容、風格、體裁的讀物，但求明白內容大意，不用花費太多時間鑽研細節，主要作用是多接觸英語，減輕對它的生疏感，鞏固以前所學過的英語，讓腦子在潛意識中吸收詞彙用法、語法結構等。

精讀，指小心認真地閱讀內容精彩、組織有條理、遣詞造句又正確的作品，着重點在於理解"準確"及"深入"，欣賞其精彩獨到之處。精讀時，可充分利用書中精心設計的練習，學習掌握有用的英語詞彙和語法知識。精讀後，可再花十分鐘朗讀其中一小段有趣的文字，邊唸邊細心領會文字的結構和意思。

《Black Cat 優質英語階梯閱讀》中的作品均值得精讀，如時間有限，不妨嘗試每兩個星期泛讀一本，輔以每星期挑選書中一章精彩的文字精讀。要學好英語，持之以恆地泛讀和精讀英文是最有效的方法。

③ 本系列的練習與測試有何功能？

《Black Cat 優質英語階梯閱讀》特別注重練習的設計，為讀者考慮周到，切合實用需求，學習功能強。每章後均配有訓練聽、說、讀、寫四項技能的練習，分量、難度恰到好處。

聽力練習分兩類，一是重聽故事回答問題，二是聆聽主角對話、書信朗讀、或模擬記者訪問後寫出答案，旨在以生活化的練習形式逐步提高聽力。每本書均配有 CD 提供作品朗讀，朗讀者都是專業演員，英國作品由英國演員錄音，美國作品由美國演員錄音，務求增加聆聽的真實感和感染力。多聆聽英式和美式英語兩種發音，可讓讀者熟悉二者的差異，逐漸培養分辨英美發音的能力，提高聆聽理解的準確度。此外，模仿錄音朗讀故事或模仿主人翁在戲劇中的對白，都是訓練口語能力的好方法。

閱讀理解練習形式多樣化，有縱橫字謎、配對、填空、字句重組等等，注重訓練讀者的理解、推敲和聯想等多種閱讀技能。

寫作練習尤具新意，教讀者使用網式圖示（spidergrams）記錄重點，採用問答、書信、電報、記者採訪等多樣化形式，鼓勵讀者動手寫作。

書後更設有升級測試（Exit Test）及答案，供讀者檢查學習效果。充分利用書中的練習和測試，可全面提升聽、説、讀、寫四項技能。

❹ 本系列還能提供甚麼幫助？

《Black Cat 優質英語階梯閱讀》提倡豐富多元的現代閱讀，巧用書中提供的資訊，有助於提升英語理解力，擴闊視野。

每本書都設有專章介紹相關的歷史文化知識，經典名著更有作者生平、社會背景等資訊。書內富有表現力的彩色插圖、繪圖和照片，使閱讀充滿趣味，部分加上如何解讀古典名畫的指導，增長見識。有的書還提供一些與主題相關的網址，比如關於不同國家的節慶源流的網址，讓讀者多利用網上資源增進知識。

Contents

CURING A COLD
傷風療法

♪♪♪♪ TWO OLD WESTERN BALLADS
美國西部懷舊歌謠

APPENDICES

The story is recorded in full. 故事錄音

🎧 This symbol indicates the exercises featured on the accompanying CD. 聽力練習的錄音標記

Mark Twain during a visit to his publisher.

Introduction

A Note on Mark Twain

Mark Twain's real name was Samuel Langhorne Clemens. He was born in Florida, Missouri, U.S.A. in 1835. When he was a young boy he lived a happy life in Hannibal, Missouri, on the Mississippi River. In 1857 he worked as a pilot on a steamboat on the Mississippi. He liked travelling on this big river.

After the American Civil War started in 1861, Mark Twain went to California to look for gold. This was the time of the California Gold Rush.

In California, Twain's life changed. He began writing stories for a San Francisco newspaper, and he changed his real name, Samuel Clemens, to Mark Twain, a pen name [1].

His short story, "The Celebrated Jumping Frog of Calaveras County", was a great success in 1865. Twain was now a famous writer. He travelled to Europe, The Holy Land and Hawaii. He wrote about his travels in *The*

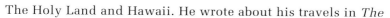

---

1. **pen name**：筆名。

9

Innocents Abroad (1869) and *Roughing It* (1872).

Twain married Olivia "Livy" Langdon, a rich woman from New England, and had three daughters. He lived in Hartford, Connecticut with his family and wrote his three great books, *The Adventures of Tom Sawyer* (1876), *Life on the Mississippi* (1883) and *The Adventures of Huckleberry Finn* (1884). In these books he remembered his youth on the Mississippi River. His other works include *The Prince and the Pauper* (1880), *A Connecticut Yankee in King Arthur's Court* (1889) and many short stories.

At the end of his life, Twain was a very sad man because he lost his

wife and two daughters. He died in 1910 at the age of seventy-five. Mark Twain was the first American writer to change the American way of writing, with his lively humour [1] and satire [2].

A Map of California's Gold Mining Camps

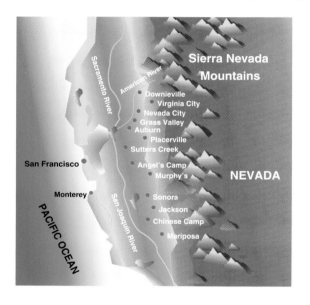

1. How many gold mining camps can you count?
2. How many rivers are there on the map?
3. What's the name of the ocean next to California?

---

1. **humour**：幽默。
2. **satire**：諷刺作品。

THE CALIFORNIA

On January 24th, 1848, John Marshall discovered gold in the American River at Sutter's Fort, California. He wasn't looking for gold. He discovered it by chance [1]!

This discovery changed the destiny of California. Suddenly, this wild territory of the Far West became world famous.

During 1849, more than 80,000 people arrived in California looking for gold. They came from the United States, Europe, Central and South America, and China. They were called "gold miners", "gold prospectors" or simply "forty-niners" [2].

---

1. **by chance**：意外地。
2. **"forty-niners"**：1849年湧到加州淘金的人。

GOLD RUSH

A lot of "forty-niners" were poor. Their dream was to find gold and "strike it rich" [1]. A lot of them found gold but only a few became very rich and important.

With the hard-working gold miners, there came saloon-keepers [2], gamblers [3], dishonest people and outlaws [4]. It was difficult to keep law and order in the Far West.

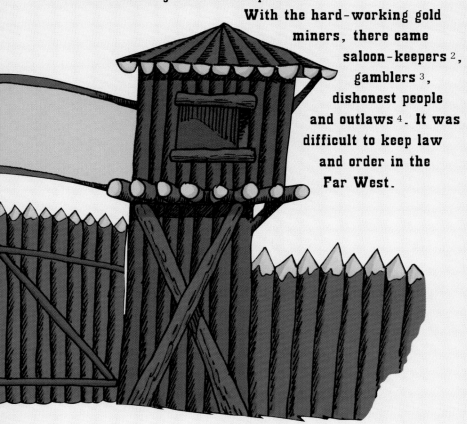

1. "strike it rich" : 賺大錢。
2. saloon-keepers : 酒吧店主。
3. gamblers : 賭徒。
4. outlaws : 犯罪後匿藏起來的人。

**Decide whether the sentences are true (T) or false (F).
Then correct the false sentences.**

		T	F
a.	John Marshall was a gold miner.	☐	☐
b.	The American River is at Sutter's Fort, California.	☐	☐
c.	The discovery of gold brought 80,000 people to California in one year.	☐	☐
d.	A gold prospector was a person who owned a gold mine.	☐	☐
e.	The forty-niners wanted to "strike it rich".	☐	☐
f.	Gamblers, dishonest people and outlaws made trouble in the Far West.	☐	☐

....

....

....

....

....

THE CELEBRATED
JUMPING FROG
OF CALAVERAS COUNTY

Before you read

Spidergram

What animal names do you know? Make a spidergram like this:

frog

1. A Letter from the East

One day a friend of mine from the East wrote me a letter. He asked me to visit an old man named Simon Wheeler. My friend wanted me to ask Simon Wheeler about a childhood companion [1], Leonidas W. Smiley.

I found Simon Wheeler

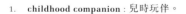

1.　**childhood companion**：兒時玩伴。

The Celebrated Jumping Frog of Calaveras County

sleeping by the stove [1] of the old tavern [2] in Angel's Mining Camp. I noticed that he was fat. His face was simple and peaceful. When he woke up, I told him that a friend of mine wanted to know about a childhood companion named Leonidas W. Smiley.

Simon Wheeler blocked me with his chair in a corner of the tavern. Then, very seriously, he began to tell me the story that follows.

There was once a fellow [3] at the mining camp named Jim Smiley. It was the winter of 1849 or maybe the spring of 1850. He was an unusual man. He always bet [4] money on anything that happened at the mining camp, and he usually won. Jim Smiley was a very lucky man. When there was a horse race, a dog-fight, [5] a cat-fight or a chicken-fight he always bet on them.

---

1. **stove** :

2. **tavern** : 酒館。

3. **fellow** : 人。
4. **bet** : 賭博。
5. **dog-fight** : 鬥狗。

A Letter from the East

1 Listen to Part One. Tick (✓) the adjectives referring to Simon Wheeler.

☐ peaceful ☐ fat ☐ crazy ☐ old ☐ lucky

Now tick the adjectives referring to Jim Smiley.

☐ young ☐ curious ☐ lucky ☐ unlucky

2 What happened in Part One?

a. Who wrote a letter to Mark Twain?
b. What did the friend ask in his letter?
c. What was Simon Wheeler doing in the old tavern?
d. Describe Simon Wheeler.
e. What did Jim Smiley bet on?
f. Why was Jim Smiley a lucky man?

3 The *Past Simple* of a verb (過去時) is often used to tell a story. Put the correct verb next to the *Past Simple*. You'll find the anagram [1] of the infinitive in the fort [2].

PAST	INFINITIVE
wrote	....
asked	....
woke	....
told	....
blocked	....
began	....
bet	....
won	....
was	....
happened	....

kas   tbe   ibeng
eawk   pehanp
nwi   llte
si   olckb   teiwr

1.   **anagram** : 變形詞 (字母排序顛倒)。   2.   **fort** : 堡壘。

4 Look at the letter Mark Twain received from his friend in the East and try to fill in the gaps using the words in the pen. Then listen and see if you were right.

California
York   remember   gold   named
about   want   Mountains   travel
visit   childhood   you
friend   live

Dear Mark,

Do you still .... me? I'm William Brown, your .... from New ....

I .... to go to California to look for .... My dream is to .... in a mining camp in the Sierra Nevada ....

Can you go to Angel's Mining Camp to .... an old man .... Simon Wheeler? Simon knows my .... friend, Leonidas W. Smiley. I want to know all .... Leonidas Smiley, before I .... to ....

Thank .... , Mark.

Your friend,
William

Before you read

Listen to Part 2. Complete the sentences with the missing words.

a. She .... wildly, ... her legs in the
air, to the sides, ... the dust, ...
and blew her nose.

b. Andrew Jackson was a .... dog and did
.... all .... long.

c. Andrew Jackson always .... the back leg of the
other dog. He didn't .... on it. He only
.... it between his .... teeth.

Now read the text and check your answers.

2. Bets and Races

Smiley owned an old horse that was slow and sick, but he won money on her. The poor horse had asthma [1] and other animal illnesses. At races she had a head start [2], because of her health problems. Near the end of every race, she became very excited and desperate [3]. She galloped [4] wildly, kicked her legs in

1. **asthma** : 哮喘。
2. **head start** : 領先。
3. **desperate** : （此處指）拼命的。
4. **galloped** : 飛奔。

the air, to the sides, raised the dust [1], coughed [2], and blew her nose. At the end of the race, she was always the happy winner.

Smiley also had a small bulldog named Andrew Jackson. Andrew Jackson was a lazy dog and did nothing all day long. But when Smiley bet money on him, he was lively and ready to fight. When there was

1. **dust** : 塵土。
2. **coughed** : 咳嗽。

Bets and Races

an important dog-fight at the mining camp, Andrew
Jackson always grabbed [1] the back leg of the other
dog. He didn't chew [2] on it. He only kept it between
his strong teeth. He didn't let go until Smiley won the
bet.

---

1. **grabbed**：（此處指）用牙咬住。
2. **chew**：咀嚼。

1 What happened in Part Two?

a. Describe Smiley's old horse.

b. Why did she have a head start at horse races?

c. What did she do at the end of every race?

d. What was the name of Smiley's lazy bulldog?

e. What did he do in order to win the dog-fights?

f. When did he let go of the other dog's back leg?

2 Match the correct parts of the sentences.

a. Smiley owned a horse that

b. At races the horse had

c. Near the end of every race

d. Smiley had a bulldog named

e. He was a lazy dog and

f. When Smiley bet money on him

1. did nothing all day long.

2. he was lively and ready to fight.

3. was slow and sick.

4. she became very excited.

5. a head start.

6. Andrew Jackson.

The main street of a typical mining town.

LIFE IN THE

From 1848 many mining camps were established in the Gold
Country: near the American River and in the Sierra Nevada
Mountains.
These camps were small settlements [1]. They were organized
quickly to meet the miners' everyday needs.
A mining camp usually had a saloon, a hotel, a stable, a
general store, an undertaker [2] and a bank.
Miners often paid for their food, drink,
clothing and other things
with gold dust or gold
nuggets [3].

1. settlements：社區。
2. undertaker：殯儀館（負責人）。
3. gold nuggets：

MINING CAMPS

Brawls [1] and fights were common, and killings were not unusual! These were tough [2] times and camps were rough [3] places.

Today a lot of camps have become ghost towns. Others have grown into towns and cities, such as Angel's Camp, Auburn, Grass Valley, Jackson, Mariposa, Nevada City, Murphy's, Placerville and Sonora. You can visit them and their abandoned [4] mines when you go to California. Take U.S. State Highway 80 to Sacramento, and then take California Highway 49 to the Gold Country.

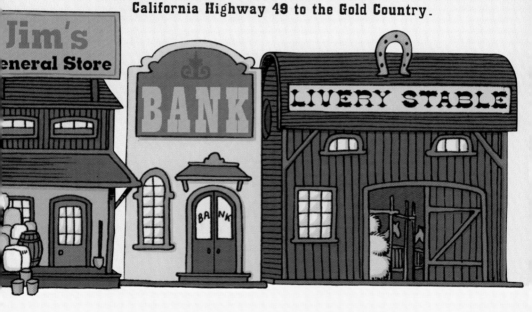

1. **brawls**：爭吵。
2. **tough**：艱苦的。
3. **rough**：危險的。
4. **abandoned**：荒廢的。

1 **Choose the correct answer.**

a. The California Gold Country is

☐ near San Francisco.

☐ in the southern part of the state.

☐ near the American River and in the Sierra Nevada Mountains.

b. The mining camps were

☐ big towns.

☐ small settlements.

☐ ghost towns.

c. Miners often paid for their food and drink

☐ with gold coins.

☐ with American dollars.

☐ with gold dust or gold nuggets.

d. Brawls and fights in the camps

☐ were common.

☐ never happened.

☐ were rare.

e. Today Angel's Camp and Grass Valley are

☐ ghost towns.

☐ abandoned cities.

☐ towns.

2 **Match the words on the left to their meaning on the right.**

a. mining camp   1. place where you keep money

b. bank   2. mine that is no longer in use

c. general store   3. place where you can sleep at night

d. stable   4. place to keep horses

e. hotel   5. small settlement near a mine

f. abandoned mine   6. place where you can buy food,
                                       clothing and other things

Before you read

Listen to Part 3. Complete the sentences with the missing words.

a. For .... months, Smiley ....
outside his house and .... his frog how to
....

b. Smiley gave .... a little .... from
behind, and Daniel Webster .... into the
.... like a doughnut.

c. Daniel .... up and .... the fly with
his long ....

d. He was .... of Daniel Webster.

Now read the text and check your answers.

31

3. Daniel Webster

Smiley found a frog one day and named it Daniel Webster. He took it home and planned to teach it a lot of things. For three months, Smiley sat outside his house and taught his frog how to jump far. Daniel Webster was a clever frog and learned quickly. Smiley gave him a little push from behind, and Daniel Webster flew into the air like a doughnut. [1] He even

---

1. **doughnut** : 油炸小圈餅。

Daniel Webster

turned one or two somersaults [1] in the air.

Smiley taught his frog to catch [2] flies [3]. "Flies, Daniel, flies!" Smiley shouted. Daniel jumped up and caught the fly with his long tongue [4].

Daniel Webster was the champion [5] jumping frog of Calaveras County. Smiley won all bets with his handsome frog. He was very proud [6] of Daniel Webster.

1. **somersaults** : 翻筋斗。
2. **catch** : 捕捉。
3. **flies** : 蒼蠅。
4. **tongue** :
5. **champion** : 冠軍。
6. **proud** : 自豪。

1 **What happened in Part Three?**

    a. What did Smiley find one day? What did he name him?

    b. Where did Smiley take Daniel?

    c. What did Smiley do for three months?

    d. How did Daniel Webster jump?

    e. What did Daniel Webster catch with his long tongue?

    f. Why was Smiley very proud of Daniel?

    g. Describe Daniel Webster.

2 **Look back at Part 2 and 3 and write the adjectives that describe Smiley's animals. Choose from the words in the gold nugget.**

sick   handsome
small   lively   clever
slow   lazy
old   champion

1 **What happened in Part Four?**

a. Where did Smiley keep Daniel Webster?

b. What did the stranger ask Smiley about his frog?

c. Why did Smiley bet forty dollars?

d. What was the stranger's answer?

e. Why did Smiley give the box to the stranger and go to the river?

f. What did the stranger do while Smiley was at the river?

2 It's a rainy day and you can't go to the river to look for gold. Here's a crossword puzzle you can do until it stops raining.

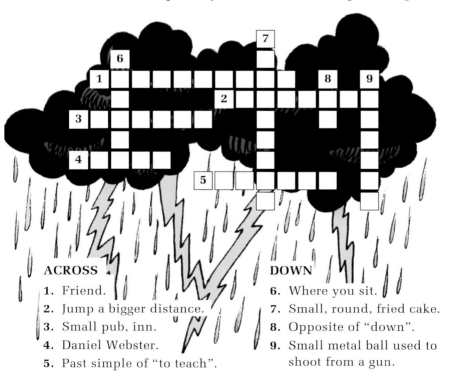

ACROSS

1. Friend.
2. Jump a bigger distance.
3. Small pub, inn.
4. Daniel Webster.
5. Past simple of "to teach".

DOWN

6. Where you sit.
7. Small, round, fried cake.
8. Opposite of "down".
9. Small metal ball used to shoot from a gun.

41

PANNING FOR GOLD

The expression "panning for gold" [1] was born during the
California Gold Rush in 1848:
The miners used a pan with a wire net on the bottom. They
separated the gold from other materials by washing them
with water. Miners usually "panned for gold" in the water
of the rivers. The
water of the river
filled their
pan with

1.   "panning for gold" : 用盆子淘金。(見圖)

sand, dirt, stones and perhaps gold dust or gold nuggets.
Other miners looked for gold in caves [1] in the Sierra Nevada
Mountains and they used a pickaxe [2]. These caves often
became gold mines.

1. caves : 洞穴。
2. pickaxe :

1 **Imagine you lived during the California Gold Rush, and fill in the spaces.**

It's April 1849. You want to go to California to look for gold.

Your name is .... You come from

.... Look at the map of California's Gold Mining

Camps on page 11 and choose the camp you prefer.

Which camp did you choose? ....

Is it near the American River, or in the Sierra Nevada Mountains?

....

Will you need a pan or a pickaxe to look for gold?

....

2 **You are at the general store of your camp, make a list of the things you need to buy.**

5. The Big Bet

After some time, Smiley returned holding a frog and said, "Now put him next to Daniel, with his front paws [1] in the same place. I'll give the word [2]!"

Then Smiley said, "One — two — three — GO!" He and the stranger pushed the frogs from behind. The new frog jumped forward, but Daniel didn't budge [3]. He tried to move his shoulders, but he was anchored [4]

---

1. **paws** : 爪。
2. **I'll give the word** : 發號令。
3. **budge** : 移動。
4. **anchored** : 繫住。

The Celebrated Jumping Frog of Calaveras County

to the floor. Smiley was very surprised and unhappy.

The stranger won the bet. "Well," he said, "I don't see anything special about this frog." He took the money and left.

Smiley looked at Daniel for a long time. Finally he said, "What has happened to Daniel? He looks terribly fat."

He caught Daniel by the back of his neck and lifted him. "Cat's alive!!! [1] You weigh five pounds [2]!"

He turned Daniel upside down [3], and the frog spit out [4] a big number of shotgun pellets.

Now he understood what happened to Daniel. Smiley was furious.

1. **"Cat's alive!"** : （美國人用的）感嘆句。

2. **five pounds** : 約2.5公斤。

3. **upside down** :

4. **spit out** : 吐出。

ARE YOU DRESSED LIKE A GOLD MINER?

Looking for gold was not easy . It was hard work from sunrise [1] to sunset [2] . Miners often worked on their knees . They needed strong work clothes . Levi Strauss was an immigrant tailor [3] at one of the mining camps . He began making work pants [4] called "blue jeans" or "Levi's" . Blue jeans became very popular in the West . Later on , Levi Strauss opened a blue-jeans factory in San Francisco . Today , in San Francisco , the Levi Strauss offices are at Levi Strauss Plaza , by the bay .

1. sunrise : 日出。
2. sunset : 日落。
3. tailor : 裁縫。
4. pants : 褲子。

51

1 **Answer these questions.**

    a. Are you wearing jeans today?

    b. What colour are they?

    c. How many people near you are wearing jeans?

    d. Why do you think jeans are so popular all over the world?

2 **Match the words below with their opposites.**

easy	native
sunset	closed
immigrant	hard
opened	weak
strong	thin
fat	sunrise

Fred, the 49'er, a gold miner

3 Can you name Fred's clothing and mining tools? Write the words
from the gold nugget in the correct places on the picture below.

blue jeans   pan
boots   hat   pickaxe
bandana   vest
shirt   belt

Animal Sounds

4 Can you identify these animals by their sounds? Listen to these animal sounds and write the number in the correct box. The first one has been done for you.

a. ☐ horse
b. ☐ cat
c. ☐ frog
d. ☐ pig
e. ☐ snake
f. ☐ sheep
g. 1 dog
h. ☐ cow
i. ☐ bird
j. ☐ chicken

5 Write a "book report" of this story.

Title ....

Author ....

Characters Major ....

Minor ....

Setting Time ....

Place ....

Short summary ....

....

....

....

....

....

FROGS

Frogs are amphibians: they can live on land and in water. Some frogs live only on land, others live only in trees and some live underground in the desert! But most frogs live in or near water. They have long hind legs that are perfect for jumping long distances. Their feet are webbed. All frogs have a long, sticky tongue to catch insects. They can croak because they have vocal chords. Adult frogs can breathe in three different ways: through their lungs, their mouth and their skin.

Tropical frogs of South America are brightly coloured and are poisonous. South American Indians extract this poison and use it to make poisonous arrows.

Choose the correct answer:

1. Frogs are called amphibians because
   ☐ they can swim.
   ☐ they can live on both land and water.
   ☐ they can jump far.

2. Most frogs live
   ☐ underground in the desert.
   ☐ in tall trees.
   ☐ in or near water.

3. Frogs can jump long distances because
   ☐ they have long hind legs.
   ☐ their feet are webbed.
   ☐ they are amphibians.

4. Their long, sticky tongue is used to
   ☐ croak.
   ☐ eat small fish.
   ☐ catch insects.

5. Frogs can breathe through
   ☐ their nose.
   ☐ their lungs, mouth and skin.
   ☐ their vocal chords.

CURING A COLD

Before you read

Listen to Part 1. Decide whether the sentences are true (T) or false (F). Then correct the false sentences.

		T	F
a.	The White House is in Virginia City, California.	☐	☐
b.	The loss of my home and happiness was not a problem.	☐	☐
c.	I am not a poet, and so I am usually an unhappy person.	☐	☐
d.	A friend told me to put my feet in cold water.	☐	☐
e.	The owner of the new restaurant took down the sign and closed the restaurant.	☐	☐
f.	A friend told me to drink a cup of warm salt water.	☐	☐
g.	There was an earthquake in California one day.	☐	☐

....
....
....
....
....

Now read the text and check your answers.

1. The First Sneeze [1]

When the White House of Virginia City, Nevada burnt down [2], I lost my home, my happiness, my health and my trunk [3]. The loss of my home and my happiness was not a problem. A home without a mother or a sister who care for [4] you isn't really a home. The loss

1. **sneeze**：打噴嚏。
2. **burnt down**：付之一炬。
3. **trunk**：
4. **care for**：關心。

Curing a Cold

of my happiness was not a problem either. I am not a poet, and so I am usually a happy person. But the loss of my good health and of my handsome trunk was a serious problem. On the day of the fire, I caught a terrible cold [1].

The first time I began to sneeze, a friend told me to put my feet in hot water and then go to bed. I did this.

The next day, another friend advised [2] me to take a cold shower. I did this too.

After an hour, another friend told me to eat a big quantity of good food. So I went to a new restaurant and started to eat everything I saw. The owner of the restaurant asked me if the people of Virginia City often had colds. I answered that they did. He then went outside, took down the new sign and closed the restaurant.

That day I met another good friend. He told me that I must drink a

1. **cold** : 傷風。
2. **advised** : 提議。

Curing a Cold

bottle of warm salt water. This was the only remedy [1] to cure [2] a cold. I tried it and the result was surprising. I threw up [3] everything I had in my stomach!

I will never drink warm salt water again! And I will never advise anyone to do so. I prefer being in a California earthquake [4], than drinking a bottle of warm salt water. This horrible remedy did not cure my cold, and it made my stomach sick for some time.

I continued to sneeze violently, to blow my nose and to destroy handkerchiefs. My suffering grew [5].

1. **remedy** : 治療法。
2. **cure** : 治療。
3. **threw up** : 吐出。
4. **earthquake** : 地震。
5. **grew** : 越來越大。

Before you read

 Listen to Part 3. Circle the word or words you hear.

a. We travelled in a *comfortable/uncomfortable* Pioneer Coach.

b. At Lake Bigler we fished and sailed on *the river/the lake*.

c. In the evening *we danced/we talked*.

d. The cold sheet-bath made my heart *freeze/stop*.

e. After a *month/week* at Lake Bigler, I decided to go to Steamboat *Sea/Springs*.

f. In San Francisco, a friend told me to drink *a glass/a bottle* of whisky every twenty-four hours.

Now read the text and check your answers.

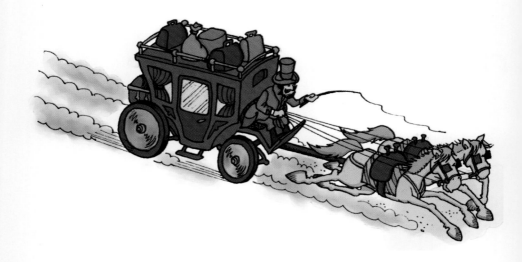

3. The San Francisco Remedy

I decided to travel to the countryside to improve my health. I went to Lake Bigler with my friend, Wilson. We travelled in a comfortable Pioneer coach 1. At Lake Bigler we fished and sailed on the lake. We hunted 2 for hours in the woods. In the evening we danced. I enjoyed myself greatly. But, my illness got worse.

1. **coach :**
2. **hunted :** 狩獵。

The San Francisco Remedy

A tourist at Lake Bigler recommended a cold sheet [1]-bath. I never refused [2] a remedy. At midnight, when it was very cold, I undressed completely. I covered my body with a wet, ice-cold sheet. I kept the sheet on my body for a long time.

It was the worst experience of my life. The wet, ice-cold sheet made my blood freeze [3] and made my heart stop! I thought it was time for me to die.

Never take a sheet-bath — NEVER! This is my advice to everyone.

1. **sheet**：牀單。
2. **refused**：拒絕。
3. **freeze**：凍至凝固。

Curing a Cold

My condition [1] got a lot worse. Other people recommended other remedies. Not one of these remedies cured my cold.

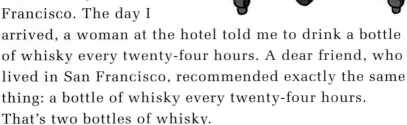

After a week at Lake Bigler, I decided to go to Steamboat Springs. I thought that the hot baths there were good for my health. They were not. While I was at Steamboat Springs, I tried several different remedies. But I just got worse and worse. I was desperate.

I finally decided to visit the city of San Francisco. The day I arrived, a woman at the hotel told me to drink a bottle of whisky every twenty-four hours. A dear friend, who lived in San Francisco, recommended exactly the same thing: a bottle of whisky every twenty-four hours. That's two bottles of whisky.

Well, I am happy to say that this San Francisco remedy finally cured my cold!

1.　**condition**：情況。

1 **What happened in Part Three?**

a. Why did Mark Twain go to Lake Bigler?

b. What did he and Wilson do at the lake?

c. What remedy did a tourist at the lake recommend?

d. How did he feel after trying this remedy?

e. Why did he go to Steamboat Springs?

f. Describe the San Francisco remedy. Did it cure his cold?

2 **Here is a list of all the remedies in this story. Put them in the correct order. Write 1, 2, 3 etc. in the boxes. Two are done for you.**

a ☐ gin, molasses and onions

b 1 feet in hot water

c ☐ two bottles of whisky

d ☐ old woman's special mixture

e 2 cold shower

f ☐ big quantity of food

g ☐ hot baths at Steamboat Springs

h ☐ trip to countryside at Lake Bigler

i ☐ cold sheet bath

j ☐ bottle of warm salt water

A CITY IS BORN

A Spanish explorer, Gaspar de Portolà, discovered San
Francisco Bay in 1769, and he built a "presidio"[1] there. At
the beginning of the 1800's, San Francisco, then called

1. "presidio"：（西班牙文）指軍事堡壘。

Yerba Buena, was a sleepy [1] Spanish village. There was a presidio, a Spanish church called Mission Dolores, and some simple homes. There were few ships in the big harbour. With the discovery of gold in 1848, everything changed. San Francisco suddenly became a busy city. In only one year, its population went from 1,000 to 30,000. Settlers came from all parts of the world.

There was a population explosion [2] in California. The new settlers needed all types of things from the industries on the East Coast. The sea route from New York to San Francisco became an important one.

The city of San Francisco became the most important settlement on the Pacific Coast. The city and its port were full of life. The gold miners often went to San Francisco to sell their gold, to buy supplies [3] and to have fun. Those were exciting times!

1. sleepy : 寂靜的。
2. population explosion : 人口爆炸。
3. supplies : (此處指) 日用品。

Here's a crossword puzzle for you to do.

ACROSS

1. Spanish word for "military fort".

2. Precious [1], yellow metal.

3. People who come to live in a place.

4. Place where ships stay.

DOWN

5. Sailing vessel [2].

6. Spanish explorer who discovered San Francisco Bay.

7. Big city on the East Coast.

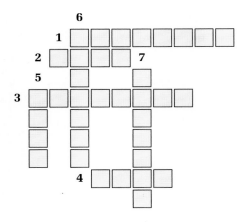

1. **precious** : 寶貴的。
2. **sailing vessel** : 船。

Clementine

In a cavern, in a canyon,
Excavating for a mine,
Dwelt a miner, a forty-niner
And his daughter Clementine.
Oh my darling, oh my darling, oh my darling
Clementine,
You are lost and gone forever
Dreadful sorry, Clementine.

Drove she ducklings [1] to the water
Every morning just at nine,
Hit her foot against a splinter
Fell into the foaming brine [2].
Oh my darling, oh my darling, oh my darling
Clementine,
You are lost and gone forever
Dreadful sorry, Clementine.

There's a churchyard, on the hillside,
Where the flowers grow and twine.
There grow roses 'mongst the posies,
Fertilized by Clementine.
Oh my darling, oh my darling, oh my darling
Clementine,
You are lost and gone forever
Dreadful sorry, Clementine.

1. **ducklings**：小鴨。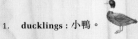
2. **brine**：（此處指）河流。

EXIT TEST

1 Comprehension

a. Who was Jim Smiley?
b. Was he lucky or unlucky? Why?
c. Who was Daniel Webster?
d. What could he do?
e. Who came to the camp one day?
f. What did Smiley suggest?
g. Where did Smiley go? Why?
h. What did the stranger do in the meantime?
i. Who won the bet? Why?

2 Context

a. Who was the author of the book?
b. What was his real name?
c. Where and when was he born?
d. Do you remember the title/s of other books of his?
e. What was the "Gold Rush" ?
f. When did it start and why?
g. What was the consequence of the discovery of gold?
h. Describe a mining camp.
i. What happens every year in May at Angel's Camp, California?
j. What is a "pan"? Why did miners use it?
k. What did miners wear?

Curing A Cold

3 Comprehension

a. What did the author lose in the fire of the White House in Virginia City?
b. What was he particularly annoyed by?
c. What did his friends advise him to do to cure his cold?
d. Whom did he meet one day? What did she suggest he could do? Did his cold pass?
e. What did he decide to do?
f. Did he like the cold sheet-bath? Was it effective as a remedy?
g. What did he do at Steamboat Springs? Did it work?
h. What eventually cured his cold?

4 Context

a. Who discovered San Francisco Bay?
b. What was built there?
c. What was San Francisco called at the beginning of 1800?
d. Was it a big city?
e. When did it change?
f. Did the population increase or decrease?
g. What did San Francisco turn into?
h. Write what you remember about San Francisco today.

5 Vocabulary

a. On a lake you usually can .... and ....

b. In the woods you can ....

c. In a restaurant you ....

d. In the Far West people .... by coach.

e. Some mining camps have become .... towns, others have grown into towns and ....

f. When you get a cold you .... violently and you .... your nose continually.

KEY TO THE ACTIVITIES AND EXIT TEST

KEY TO THE ACTIVITIES

A Map of California's Gold Mining Camps

Page 11

1. 13
2. 3
3. the Pacific Ocean

True or False

Page 14

a. F – John Marshall discovered gold by chance.
b. T
c. F – More than 80,000 people arrived in California.
d. F – A gold prospector was a person who looked for gold.
e. T
f. T

Page 20 – Exercise 1

Simon Wheeler – fat, peaceful, old
Jim Smiley – curious, lucky

Page 20 – Exercise 2

a. A friend from the East.
b. To visit an old man named Simon Wheeler.

c. He was sleeping.
d. He was fat and his face was simple and peaceful.
e. Anything that happened at the mining camp.
f. Because he usually won.

Page 20 – Exercise 3

write, ask, wake, tell, block, begin, bet, win, is, happen

Page 21 – Exercise 4

remember, friend, York, want, gold, live, Mountains, visit, named, childhood, about, travel, California, you

Before you read

Page 22

a. galloped / kicked / raised / coughed
b. lazy / nothing / day
c. grabbed / chew / kept / strong

Page 26 – Exercise 1

a. She was old, slow and sick.
b. Because of her health problems.

c. She became excited and desperate and won the race.

d. His name was Andrew Jackson.

e. He always grabbed the back leg of the other dog.

f. When Smiley won the bet.

Page 26 – Exercise 2

a. 3. **d.** 6.
b. 5. **e.** 1.
c. 4. **f.** 2.

Page 30 – Exercise 1

a. near the American River and in the Sierra Nevada Mountains.
b. small settlements.
c. with gold dust or gold nuggets.
d. were common.
e. towns.

Page 31 – Exercise 2

a. 5. **d.** 4.
b. 1. **e.** 3.
c. 6. **f.** 2.

Before you read

Page 31

a. three / sat / taught / jump / far
b. him / push / flew / air
c. jumped / caught / tongue
d. very / proud

Page 34 – Exercise 1

a. He found a frog and named it Daniel Webster.
b. He took Daniel home.
c. He taught Daniel to jump far.

d. He jumped like a doughnut and turned somersaults.

e. He caught flies.

f. Because he was the champion jumping frog of Calaveras County.

g. He was small, green, handsome, and very clever.

Page 34 – Exercise 2

sick
slow
old

small
lively
lazy

clever
handsome
champion

Page 35 – Exercise 3

a. found
b. taught / jump
c. gave
d. flew
e. turned
f. won

Before you read

Page 37

a. 4 / **b.** 1 / **c.** 3 / **d.** 5 / **e.** 2

Page 41 – Exercise 1

a. He kept him in a box with small holes in it.

b. "What's he good for?"

c. He bet forty dollars that his frog could outjump any frog in Calaveras County.

d. He said that he couldn't bet because he didn't have a frog.

e. To find a frog for the stranger.

f. He put some shotgun pellets into the frog's mouth.

e. lots of shotgun pellets.

f. furious.

g. forty dollars.

Page 50 – Exercise 3

receive, letter, Mining, found, lots of, companion, name, miner, happens, frog, jumper, wins, stranger, lost, forty-dollar, take, meet

Page 41 – Exercise 2

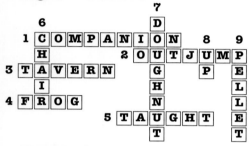

Page 44 – Exercise 1, 2

Open answers.

Page 48 – Exercise 1

a. Smiley brought a frog from the river.

b. He put the new frog next to Daniel.

c. Daniel didn't move.

d. Because Daniel couldn't move – he was anchored to the floor.

e. Because he was full of shotgun pellets.

f. He spit out a big number of shotgun pellets.

Page 49 – Exercise 2

a. a frog.

b. jumped forward.

c. move his shoulders.

d. fat.

Page 52 – Exercise 1

Open answers.

Page 52 – Exercise 2

easy - hard
sunset - sunrise
immigrant - native
opened - closed
strong - weak
fat - thin

Page 53 – Exercise 3

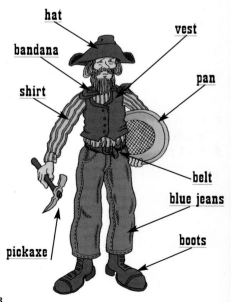

hat

vest

bandana

pan

shirt

belt

blue jeans

boots

pickaxe

Page 54 – Exercise 4

a. 3		**f.** 6	
b. 7		**g.** 1	
c. 2		**h.** 9	
d. 4		**i.** 5	
e. 10		**j.** 8	

Page 55 – Exercise 5

Open answers.

Frogs

Page 56

1. they can live on both land and water.
2. in or near water.
3. they have long hind legs.
4. catch insects.
5. their lungs, mouth and skin.

Before you read

Page 58

a. F – The White House is in Virginia City, Nevada.
b. T
c. F – I am not a poet, and so I am usually a happy person.
d. F – A friend told me to put my feet in hot water.
e. T
f. F – A friend told me to drink a bottle of warm salt water.
g. F – I prefer being in a California earthquake.

Page 63 – Exercise 1

a. He lost his home, his happiness, his health and his trunk.
b. Because a home without a mother or a sister who care for you isn't really a home.
c. No, it wasn't.
d. Putting his feet in hot water and then going to bed; taking a cold shower.
e. He ate everything he saw.
f. The bottle of warm salt water.

Page 63 – Exercise 2

hot - cold
without - with
happy - unhappy
good - bad
everything - nothing
outside - inside
open - shut
sick - well
new - old
big - small

Page 64 – Exercise 3

a. his home, his happiness, his health and his trunk.
b. he's not a poet.
c. feet in hot water.
d. often had colds.
e. threw up.

Before you read

Page 65

a. F – The old woman came from a deserted part of the Far West.
b. F – She prepared a special mixture of molasses, aquafortis, oils and other strange drugs.
c. T

d. F – I coughed every moment of the day and of the night.

e. T

f. T

g. F – Gin and molasses did not cure my cold.

Page 69 – Exercise 1

a. She came from a deserted part of the Far West.

b. She prepared a mixture of molasses, aquafortis, oils and other strange drugs.

c. He felt mean and dangerous.

d. He felt a lot worse.

e. Because he coughed every moment of the day and night.

f. His breath smelt terrible.

Page 69 – Exercise 2

B	R	H	I	M	L	T	N	G	S
M	X	F	Q	B	C	O	Q	A	B
R	M	N	M	V	Z	L	L	Q	G
H	O	I	L	S	V	K	N	U	M
F	L	C	K	Y	W	J	H	A	N
O	A	Z	W	E	T	V	C	F	S
U	S	A	C	S	J	O	A	O	C
Z	S	T	B	H	S	F	P	R	P
Y	E	U	D	R	U	G	S	T	A
P	S	V	O	R	B	E	Y	I	R
O	T	C	F	X	P	G	W	S	P

Page 70 – Exercise 3

a. seemed

b. isolated

c. practice / ill

d. made / unusual

e. had

f. mad

g. head

Before you read

Page 71

a. comfortable

b. lake

c. danced

d. stop

e. week / Springs

f. a bottle

Page 75 – Exercise 1

a. To improve his health.

b. They fished, sailed and hunted.

c. A cold sheet-bath.

d. He thought he was going to die!

e. Because he thought that the hot baths were good for his health.

f. The San Francisco remedy was a bottle of whisky every twenty-four hours. Yes, it cured his cold.

Page 75 – Exercise 2

a 6

b 1

c 10

d 5

e 2

f 3

g 9

h 7

i 8

j 4

Crossword puzzle

Page 78

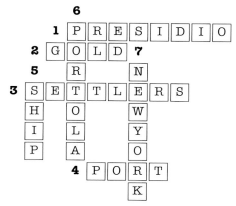

Circle the adjectives

Page 81

unusual
international
friendly
beautiful
exciting
extraordinary
unforgettable
modern
colourful

Page 84 – Exercise 1

a. A man who lived in a mining camp.
b. He was lucky.
c. Smiley's frog.
d. He could jump far, he could turn somersaults and he could catch flies with his long tongue.
e. A stranger.
f. He suggested that they have a bet on whose frog could jump the furthest.
g. He went down to the river to find a frog for the stranger.
h. He put some shotgun pellets into Daniel Webster's mouth.
i. The stranger won the bet because Daniel Webster couldn't move as he was so full of shotgun pellets.

Page 84 – Exercise 2

a. Mark Twain.
b. Samuel Langhorne Clemens.
c. He was born in Florida, Missouri in 1835.
d. *The Innocents Abroad, Roughing It, The Adventures of Tom Sawyer, Life on the Mississippi, The Adventures of Huckleberry Finn, The Prince and the Pauper, A Connecticut Yankee in King Arthur's Court.*
e. The Gold Rush was when more than 80,000 people

arrived in California looking for gold.

f. It started in 1849 after John Marshall discovered gold in the American River at Sutter's Fort, California.

g. People came from all over the world to live in the Far West.

h. *Possible answer:*
They were small settlements and usually had a saloon, a hotel, a stable, a general store, an undertaker and a bank. The camps were rough places and there was often a lot of fighting.

i. There is a frog competition.

j. It was a sort of plate with a wire net in the bottom. Miners used it to look for gold in the rivers.

k. They wore jeans, boots, a hat and a bandana.

Page 84 – Exercise 3

a. He lost his home, his happiness, his health and his trunk.

b. The loss of his good health and his trunk.

c. To put his feet in hot water and go to bed, to eat a lot of food, drink a bottle of warm salt water.

d. He met a very old woman who suggested that he drank a special mixture of molasses, acquafortis, oils and other drugs. His cold

didn't pass – the mixture made him crazy.

e. He decided to travel to the countryside to improve his health.

f. No, he didn't. He thought he was going to die.

g. He tried the hot baths, but they didn't work.

h. Drinking two bottles of whisky a day.

Page 84 – Exercise 4

a. Gaspar de Portilà, a Spanish explorer.

b. A presidio.

c. Yerba Buena.

d. No, it was a small village.

e. It changed with the discovery of gold in 1848.

f. It increased.

g. It turned into a busy city.

h. *Possible answer:*
It is an international commercial and banking centre. There's a large Chinese neighbourhood called Chinatown. There are excellent museums and universities. The city is built on steep hills.

Page 85 – Exercise 5

a. fish / sail
b. hunt
c. eat
d. travelled
e. ghost / cities
f. sneeze / blow

Notes

BLACK CAT ENGLISH CLUB
Membership Application Form

BLACK CAT ENGLISH CLUB is for those who love English reading and seek for better English to share and learn with fun together.

Benefits offered: - *Membership Card*

                     - *Member badge, poster, bookmark*

                     - *Book discount coupon*

                     - *Black Cat English Reward Scheme*

                     - *English learning e-forum*

                     - *Surprise gift and more...*

Simply fill out the application form below and fax it back to 2565 1113.

Join Now! It's FREE exclusively for readers who have purchased *Black Cat English Readers* !

The book(or book set) that you have purchased: _____

English Name:_____ (Surname) _____ (Given Name)

Chinese Name: _____

Address: _____

Tel: _____ Fax: _____

Email:_____
                                 (Login password for e-forum will be sent to this email address.)

Sex: ❑ Male   ❑ Female

Education Background: ❑ Primary 1-3   ❑ Primary 4-6   ❑ Junior Secondary Education (F1-3)

                          ❑ Senior Secondary Education (F4-5)   ❑ Matriculation

                          ❑ College   ❑ University or above

Age: ❑ 6 - 9   ❑ 10 - 12   ❑ 13 - 15   ❑ 16 - 18   ❑ 19 - 24   ❑ 25 - 34

       ❑ 35 - 44   ❑ 45 - 54   ❑ 55 or above

Occupation: ❑ Student   ❑ Teacher   ❑ White Collar   ❑ Blue Collar

                 ❑ Professional   ❑ Manager   ❑ Business Owner   ❑ Housewife

                 ❑ Others (please specify: _____)

As a member, what would you like **BLACK CAT ENGLISH CLUB** to offer:

      ❑ Member gathering/ party   ❑ English class with native teacher   ❑ English competition

      ❑ Newsletter   ❑ Online sharing   ❑ Book fair

      ❑ Book discount   ❑ Others (please specify: _____)

Other suggestions to **BLACK CAT ENGLISH CLUB**:

_____

                                  Please sign here: _____

                                      (Date:_____)